Puffin Books
Editor: Kaye Webb

Tales of Joe and Timothy

Joe lived right at the top of a high, high house with his
father and mother and Charlie-boy the budgie, and
Timothy lived right at the bottom of a high, high house
with his father and mother and Alfie the cat (and later on
a baby sister as well). The boys often met each other
in the playground at the park, and they liked each other
very much, but they didn't discover until the day they
both went exploring the middle of their tall house on the
same day, that they had been living at the top and the
bottom of the same house all this time!
Of course, after that they played together in each other's
homes and in the playground almost every day. They
seemed to have many more interesting things to do and
see now, such as the time they saw Joe's
Dad at work laying pipes in the road, and Timothy's Dad
working on a high building, *and* having a ride in Jessie's
Dad's bus. It really was very exciting living in the high,
high house, they thought, when it was so full of people
who did such interesting things.
The author, Dorothy Edwards, is best known for her
inimitable 'Naughty Little Sister' stories, which we
publish in Young Puffins as *My Naughty Little Sister*, *My
Naughty Little Sister's Friends* and *When My Naughty
Little Sister Was Good*.
For reading aloud to children of three to six.

Tales of
Joe and Timothy

Dorothy Edwards

Illustrated by Reintje Venema

Puffin Books

Puffin Books, Penguin Books Ltd,
Harmondsworth, Middlesex, England
Penguin Books Australia Ltd, Ringwood, Victoria, Australia
Penguin Books Canada Ltd, 41 Steelcase Road West,
Markham, Ontario, Canada
Penguin Books (N.Z.) Ltd, 182–190 Wairau Road,
Auckland 10, New Zealand

First published by Methuen 1969
Published in Puffin Books 1974
Reprinted 1975

Text copyright © Dorothy Edwards, 1969

Illustrations copyright © Methuen & Co Ltd, 1969

Made and printed in Great Britain by
Richard Clay (The Chaucer Press) Ltd, Bungay, Suffolk

Set in Monotype Bembo

For Helen Angela Brunt, and her Daddy, with love

Contents

Making friends

There are two little boys who live in a big, smoky city full of houses and shops and factories, and streets where cars and lorries and buses and motor-bikes go up and down, down and up all the time, and stations where trains rush in and out day and night, and where there is always noise, *noise*, NOISE.

One of these boys is called Joe, and he lives right up at the TOP of a very tall house, with his Dad and his Mum and a pet budgie called Charlie-boy.

They live so high up that they can walk right out of their kitchen window on to a flat roof-top. That is where Joe's Mum hangs her washing out to dry, and his Dad grows tomatoes in a little glasshouse among the chimneys!

The other boy is called Timothy, and he lives right at the very BOTTOM of a very tall house with *his* Mum and Dad and a cat called Alfie. They live so far down that they have to go up steps to get to the roadway and the little backyard, where Timothy's Mum hangs her washing, and his Dad keeps rabbits in a wooden hutch by the coal-bins.

Joe and Timothy aren't old enough to go to school, and as there isn't much room for them to play at home, they used to get very fidgetty, so their mothers had to take them out in the afternoons. Sometimes they went to the shops, but mostly they went to the Park, especially in summertime.

This Park is the nicest place in the city. It is really a big, big garden full of trees and flowers, where there are tidy paths to walk on, and seats for sitting down on. At one end there is a fountain with goldfish and a pretty rock-garden. That is where Joe's mother liked to sit.

At the other end of the Park is a place where people play tennis behind wire-netting, and golf on a little bumpy course with tin holes and flags in it, and Timothy's mother used to like to sit there.

Now, in the middle of the Park there is a playground, with a paddling pool, and a sandpit, and swings and round-and-round things, and climbing-frames for children to play on.

Sometimes there is a Special Lady who comes to this playground to teach the not-at-school children games and songs, and to tell them stories. It is the place that Joe and Timothy liked best. So as soon as their mothers were nicely settled they always went to the playground.

One day, Joe saw a nice, friendly little boy in a red jersey playing in the playground, and he smiled at him. Timothy saw a nice, friendly little boy in a brown coat playing in the playground, and he smiled too. The boy in the red jersey was Timothy, the boy in the brown coat was Joe, and they were soon paddling and swinging and climbing together like old friends. And they both said how nice it was to have someone to play with and to sing the Special Lady's songs with.

There is a big clock over the playground, and Joe knows how to tell the time. So his Mum would say, 'When the clock says half past four, you must come and find me, and we will go home to get Daddy's tea.'

Timothy couldn't tell the time, so his Mum would come to fetch him. She always fetched him at a quarter to five.

Whenever Joe went to the Park he looked for Timothy. When Timothy went to the Park he looked for Joe. They became very good friends. Joe told Timothy all about his home high up among the chimney tops and about his budgie, Charlie-boy, and Timothy told Joe about his home down below the street and about his cat, Alfie.

Joe said, 'I'd like to see your home under the street, Timothy,' and Timothy said, 'I should like to see where you live among the chimney-pots, Joe.'

Then they would laugh and race each other up to the top of the climbing-frame, and sing their favourite Special Lady's song. They would sing:

'Oh, the grand old Duke of York
He had ten thousand men –
He marched them up to the top of the hill,
And he marched them down again.
And when they were up – they were up,
And when they were down – they were down,
And when they were only half-way up
They were neither up nor down.'

What a surprise!

Joe lives right on top of a high, high house with his father and mother and Charlie-boy the budgie, and Timothy lives right at the bottom of a high, high house with his father and mother and Alfie the cat. They are both friendly, happy boys and like their homes very much.

When the weather was bad and they couldn't go out they tried not to make too much fuss, because they knew that when they could go out again they might be lucky enough to go to the playground, and if they went to the playground they might see each other. It made so much difference now they were friends.

One day however, a nasty thing happened. Poor Joe woke up with spots all over himself and a funny feeling in his head, and the lady-doctor who climbed all the way up the stairs to see him said he had measles. Poor Joe! He had to stay indoors, even though the weather was nice, and that made him very miserable.

And would you believe it, Timothy was miserable too, because *he* had woken up with spots as well, and *his* head felt funny, and the gentleman-doctor who went to see him said he had measles, too!

I suppose they must have caught it at the same time.

When Joe got up, and saw the sunshine dancing on all

the roofs that were lower than theirs, he grew very bored and cross. He said, 'Oh, what will my friend Timothy think if I'm not at the playground?'

And when Timothy got up he wondered about Joe. He said, 'I hope Joe won't forget me'.

Well now, it wasn't long before Joe felt much better,

and tired of having to stay at home. He thought, 'I know! I can't go outdoors yet, but I *can* take a walk through the house. Why, that would be quite an adventure!'

Now Joe had walked down the stairs lots of times with his Mum or his Dad, but of course it isn't an adventure unless you do it on your own, is it? So, without saying a word, Joe opened the door: and there were the steep stairs going down, down, down.

So, down, down, down went Joe. On every landing there was a door; and when he came to a door he remembered to walk very, very quietly, so as not to disturb anyone; but when he was on the staircase part he sang a little song that the Special Lady had taught the children to sing in the playground.

On that very same day, Joe's friend Timothy was feeling better too. He was so tired of looking out of the window and seeing people's feet going by on the pavement above his head that *he* decided to have an indoor adventure, too! He decided it would be fun to go outside and climb all the way up through the house.

Now Timothy had never been upstairs in the house before because his family had a special under-the-pavement front door with steps up to the roadway; but there was a door at the back of his mother's bedroom that opened into the house, so he went through that.

The first thing he saw was the staircase going up, up, up. So *up* he went. It *was* a climb! Up and up.

On to a landing and softly past a door went Timothy, and as he climbed the stairs he sang too. *He* sang one of the Special Lady's songs. He sang:

'Oh, the grand old Duke of York
He had ten thousand men –
He marched them up to the top of the hill,
And he marched them down again . . .'

Then Timothy stopped singing for a moment, because he was coming to a landing, but, do you know, the *song* didn't stop. It went on – like this – soft at first but getting louder and louder:

'. . . up to the top of the hill
And he marched them down again.
And when they were UP – they were UP,
And when they were DOWN
              – they were DOWN
And when they were only half-way up
They were neither up nor down.'

And Joe looked down, and Timothy looked up!

And there they were! They had been living in the same house all the time, and they hadn't known it. They *were* pleased to see each other!

They sat down on the stairs side by side and told each other about their measles.

Then Joe said, 'Now you will be able to visit my upstairs home, and I can visit your downstairs home. Won't that be nice?'

And that was just what did happen.

Now when the boys go to the Park, sometimes Joe's Mum takes them, and sometimes Timothy's. Sometimes they go with both mothers together. When both mothers go they have to take it in turns to sit in their own favourite parts of the Park, but of course Joe and Timothy go straight to the playground.

The wind and the tickly vest

After Joe and Timothy had found out that they had both been living in the same house all the time, Timothy went to visit Joe's home high among the chimney-pots.

Joe showed him the roof where his Mum hung her washing and his Dad grew tomatoes. He showed him a hole in the brickwork that you can look through and see all the roofs and chimneys of the town away below. You can see a bit of the railway line too, and sometimes there is a train. You can see the gasworks with the big round towers. Sometimes these towers are very high, sometimes they will be quite low.

Joe says he has never seen these towers moving, so he thinks they must be magic.

Timothy often looked at the gasworks towers after that, and he never saw them moving either.

Now, one day Joe's Mum went shopping and brought home some nice warm woolly vests for Joe's Dad to wear. They were lovely thick vests, and she thought they would keep his Dad really warm when he was at work. Joe's father works out of doors. He helps to make big holes in the road and lay pipes in them, and that is a very cold job in winter-time.

Joe's father was very pleased when he saw the new vests, and because it was chilly he wore one to work the very next day.

But oh dear! When he came home that night, he said, 'I can't wear that vest anymore; it's too tickly!' He said, 'It made me itch and itch!'

And he pulled such a funny face and moved his shoulders in such an itchy way that Joe laughed and his mother laughed too.

Then Joe's Mum said, 'Oh dear, I was afraid that would happen. You know what very tender skin you have – just like Joe's.'

Joe looked at his father, and his father looked at Joe and they laughed all over again then.

Then his mother said, 'You *would* wear that vest

straight away. You should have let me wash it first in my nice soft washing stuff, then it wouldn't be tickly at all.'

So his Dad said, 'Well, if that's all, get me a vest washed as soon as possible, for I certainly need a warm vest this weather.' And he took off the tickly vest and put on one of his old ones again.

Joe's Mum washed the tickly vests – there were three of them – and she went out of the kitchen window and pegged them on to her clothes line. At once the wind got inside them, and they blew and blew.

It was such a blowy day they began to dry at once. They looked so funny blowing on the line high up above other people's chimney-pots, up against the sky.

Joe and Timothy watched them flapping. First they went up into the air – just as if they were surprised; then they went straight out – as if they were saying, 'How nice to see you,' to the gasworks' towers. Then they went this way, that way, this way, that way. Flap, flap, flap, flap!

Joe and Timothy waved their arms about and pretended to be vests on the line. It was very exciting. The wind blew stronger and stronger, and the vests flapped faster and faster. Then, all of a sudden, flap, flap, and

away – the naughty wind pulled one of the vests right off the line. The pegs fell down, and off it went – away and away!

'Oh, it's like a bird,' said Joe.

'No. No. It's a parachute; a parachute!' called Timothy.

'Oh dear, oh dear, there goes your Dad's new woolly vest!' cried Joe's mother.

But the vest didn't go very far, after all. It sailed, and stopped – and dropped. Down and down, round and round. And it fell right into the gasworks' yard. They all watched it: Joe and Timothy through the brickwork hole, and Joe's mother over the top of the wall.

'We shall have to go and get it,' Joe's Mum said, and, as she was minding Timothy that morning, she said he must go too.

So they put on their hats and their coats and went down through the tall house and out into the windy street, down the road and round a very blowy corner until they came to the gasworks.

The wall round the gasworks was so high the boys couldn't see the towers from where they were. There was a big wooden gateway in the wall, with a little hut inside where the gate-keeper sat.

Joe's Mum told the man in the little hut all about the flying vest, and the man laughed and laughed. But he was a kind man, so he called another man and asked him to take them round to the yard to look for themselves.

They went into the yard where there were heaps and heaps of black shiny coal and grey knobby coke, and men with coaly faces pushing little trucks and digging with shovels.

'There it is!' cried Timothy almost at once. And there it was, indeed! One of the men had just picked it up, and was looking at it in a very astonished way.

He told Joe's Mum that he had seen it coming out of the sky. He said, 'I thought at first it was a swan – or a seagull.' (Joe had said it looked like a bird, hadn't he?)

Joe's mother was very glad to get it back, even though it had got very dirty falling on to the coals and had to be rubbed and rubbed before it was washed clean again.

She hung it up with four pegs next time, and as the wind was still blowing it dried very quickly, and so did the other vests.

When Joe's father came home, there was a nice, clean, soft, new woolly vest for him to wear! And those vests didn't feel a bit tickly after that, either!

On the landing

When Joe's and Timothy's mothers first heard about them going out on the stairs on their own they had been cross, but, as time went on and as they were always wanting to see each other, their mothers said at last that they could go through the big house on their own, providing they were quiet, and careful, and never, never went out of doors.

Joe and Timothy are sensible little boys so they promised to be careful and good, and they kept their promise. After that they used the staircase on their own every day. They were so well-behaved that the other people in the house hardly noticed them. And if they did, they only thought, 'What nice, good children!'

After a while they began to meet on the half-way landing where there was a big window. When they met they would sit on the floor and whisper together to decide what games they would play that morning. The games they played upstairs were different from the ones they played downstairs. When they had made up their minds they would go and tell one mother that they were going to play at the other mother's home.

Wasn't that a good idea?

Well now, one day when they were sitting on the landing floor, pushing their toy cars very quietly with their hands while they decided whether to play a dirty game like coal-miners in Timothy's backyard where the coal-bins were, or do a jig-saw on Joe's bedroom floor, Timothy said, 'Joe, I think someone's peeping!'

Joe looked all around but he couldn't see anyone. There was no one about. But Timothy said, 'I think I saw an eye looking through that letter-box.' He pointed to the landing door.

Joe looked, but the letter-box was shut.

'I didn't see any eye,' Joe whispered. 'Come on,' he said, 'let's be coal-miners today,' so off they went.

The next day when they met on the landing, Timothy showed Joe a new book his Gran had sent him. There was a picture of a funny man on the cover. This funny man was running after a bus. He must have been very late getting up because he had a boot on his head instead of a hat,

27

and a hat on his foot instead of a boot, and his coat was on back to front, and, as he ran, all sorts of strange things were falling out of his pockets: oranges, and coconuts and scissors and flower-pots – even a little black piggy!

This picture made them laugh, though of course they had to laugh quietly. As they laughed, Joe heard a little sound, and he was just in time to see the letter-box closing.

Nothing else happened, even though they both crept over to the door to look, so they went off together to look at the pictures in Timothy's new book.

Still, it was very strange, wasn't it? The two little boys wondered and wondered about it all that day. 'What could it have been?' they said.

Well, they soon found out. The very next day, when they sat down to talk, Joe told Timothy that his Dad had brought him home some toffees for being a good boy. He had them in his pocket to share with Timothy.

He took the bag out of his pocket, and Timothy took one, and then Joe had one himself.

The toffees were wrapped in rather sticky paper, and as the Special Lady in the park had taught them a song about not leaving paper around, they didn't know what to do with their toffee-papers.

Then Joe had a silly-billy funny idea. He stuck his sticky paper on his nose. That made him look very comic indeed! So Timothy stuck *his* toffee-paper on his nose and he looked comic too.

Joe said, 'Hello, Mr Funny-Man,' to Timothy.

Timothy said, 'Hello, Mr Toffee-nose,' to Joe, and he said it in a little squeaky voice, and this made them both laugh so much they had to put their hands in front of their mouths so as not to disturb anyone.

But someone else was laughing too. Not quietly either, out loud as loud: 'Ha, ha, ha, he-he-he!' – like that.

The two little boys had been so busy with their toffees and their fun that they hadn't seen the door with the letter-box opening. Now they both turned round quickly.

There stood a little brown girl, with red bows in her hair, laughing and laughing at them. She laughed so much she fell 'plop' on the floor!

'Funny boys, funny boys!' she said.

Joe and Timothy laughed out loud too, then, and soon the three children were rolling and rolling all over the floor, laughing and laughing.

Every time they stopped someone said, 'Hello, Mr

Funny Man,' or 'Hello, Mr Toffee-nose,' or 'Funny boys,' and they laughed all over again.

Then Joe gave the little brown girl one of his toffees, and they all stuck papers on their noses.

They did enjoy themselves!

After that, the little brown girl often came out to talk to Joe and Timothy when they met on the landing.

She had some brothers and sisters who went to school, and she told Joe and Timothy all about them.

Joe and Timothy told her all about the Park and the playground where they had first seen each other, and about their friend, the Special Lady.

The little girl was very interested. She said, 'I should just like to see that playground, and that lovely Special Lady of yours!'

So Joe and Timothy asked their mothers if, the next time they went to the Park, the little girl could come as well. Their Mums thought this was a good idea.

Timothy's Mum said, 'I thought that the little girl looked lonely. Her mother told me that the other children are out all day at school, and her husband comes in at different times. I don't suppose she has time to take the little girl to the Park herself.'

Timothy's mother said she would speak to the little

girl's mother straight away, and they could all go to the
Park together that very afternoon.

And that very afternoon, while Timothy's mother was
getting herself and Timothy ready downstairs, Joe and
his Mum stopped on the middle landing to call for the
little brown girl.

The little girl and her mother were already waiting.
She was jumping up and down, she was so pleased, and
she had lovely new blue ribbons in her hair that jumped
too!

Her mother was very happy. She smiled and smiled,
and said that sometimes, when she could manage it, she'd
like to come along to the Park as well. But she said she'd

have to leave early so as to get the tea for the school-children.

So now, when Joe and Timothy go to the Park, the little brown girl often goes with them, and sometimes her Mum goes too, and, if she has to leave early, she lets the little girl stay behind in the playground, because she knows that Joe and Timothy will look after her, and that their Mums will bring her safely home.

She says, 'I know my Jessie is all right when she has such nice, well-behaved boys to play with!'

And now you know that the little brown girl's name is Jessie!

Jessie and Lady Peg

When the weather is bad, Joe and Timothy and Jessie can't get to the Park. If they do go out it is only to the shops, and then their mothers are in such a hurry to get home again that it is hardly like an outing at all. The children don't like this sort of going-out.

There was a time once when it rained and rained, day after day. It was so wet that the roof outside the kitchen window of Joe's home had become one big puddle, and Joe's Dad had had to go out on to it in his working boots, and scoop up the water with a tin and empty it into a bucket, and hand the bucket through to Joe's Mum to empty down the sink. He had to do this over and over again before he could open his greenhouse!

It rained so much that the dusty, coaly water in the little downstairs yard collected together and ran down the steps to Timothy's home-door, and then it crept under the door, and along the little passage, so that his Mum had to mop it up with a big cloth!

It was so wet that the walls on the staircase and landings were all steamy-looking.

On one of these wet days Joe and Timothy went upstairs from Timothy's home to look for Jessie, and they found her outside her door, playing a very funny game.

Jessie was putting her hands against the steamy-looking walls, and when she took them away she left two little wet hand-shapes on the wall!

Joe and Timothy thought this was a very interesting game so they pressed their hands on to the wall too! Then Jessie made handmarks on another part of the wall, and so did Joe, and so did Timothy, until there were lots of little damp hand-marks all round the landing. But they soon got tired of playing this game.

'Oh dear,' said Joe, 'I wish it wouldn't rain. I wish we could go to the Park.'

'I expect the swings are soaking wet,' said Timothy.

'I expect the climbing up-and-down frames and the round-and-rounds are wet as well,' said Joe.

'I expect the Park Keeper is wet too,' said funny Jessie. 'I expect his hat is all soaking and dripping and his coat is all runny with wet. I expect he looks very funny!'

'I hope the Special Lady isn't wet though,' said Joe.

'No, she won't be wet,' said Jessie. 'That Special Lady has a lovely shiny red mac, and a red mac hat, and white Wellingtons, and a green umbrella! I saw her when I went out with my Mum yesterday. That Special Lady always looks so nice!'

'I wish we could make the rain stop,' sighed Timothy. 'Oh dear!'

'Oh dear!' said Joe.

But Jessie didn't say 'oh dear' – she is a clever child and full of ideas.

'I know,' she said, 'you can come with me to take some fish-heads to Lady Peg,' and she popped back into her home, and came out with a little newspaper parcel.

Joe and Timothy didn't know anything about Lady Peg; but they waited for Jessie to come out, and then followed her downstairs to the landing below.

'Round the corner and down this passage,' said Jessie. She had yellow ribbons on today, and they bobbed and bobbed as she skipped along. 'Round here, boys!' she called.

Past closed doors they went, and then – there was a door that was wide open, and, sitting outside the door under a landing window with a little table in front of her, was a tiny old lady.

This tiny old lady had a woolly cap on her head, and funny old-fashioned glasses on her nose, and she was needleworking away on a little piece of cloth.

'Is that Lady Peg?' whispered Timothy.

The little brown girl shook her head. 'Hello, Miss Emily,' she said.

The old lady looked up and peered at them. Then she said, 'Hello, Jessie.' And she looked at Joe and Timothy and said, 'And these must be Joe and Timothy.'

Tiny little old Miss Emily lives in a little room that is so full of boxes and bits that she finds it easier to sit outside her own door when she is at work. She stitches badges and decorations for the uniforms of very high-up soldiers and sailors and airmen, and the boxes are full of the odds and ends she uses for her work.

Jessie had often visited her and looked into her boxes, but Joe and Timothy had never been there before.

'We had herrings for breakfast, and Mum saved the heads for Lady Peg,' said Jessie.

'That was very kind of her,' the old lady said. 'As you are here, you can give them to her. You will find her plate on the sideboard.'

Jessie squeezed past the old lady, and the little boys followed. Inside, the little room was full of furniture, all pressed together, with boxes and parcels piled up on it. In the middle was a little bed with a smart patchwork cover, and on the cover was a lovely big, smoky-blue cat with a white chest, curled up and sleepy-looking.

When this cat saw Jessie it said, 'Mow' and it stood up very slowly and stretched itself with its feet out, and then it jumped off the bed and began to rub itself round and round Jessie's little brown legs.

'Look, Lady Peg,' said Jessie, 'I've brought your dinner!'

Joe and Timothy looked for the plate that Miss Emily had told them about, and Jessie undid her parcel and put three fish-heads on the plate.

'There,' she said, 'that's for your dinner, and some more for tea later.'

'Mow!' said the smoky-blue cat again, and then she began to eat her dinner.

How she enjoyed it! She put one paw on the edge of the plate while she ate and ate, and when she had eaten it all up, she walked in and out of the children's legs, Jessie's, Joe's, and Timothy's, waving her tail and saying, 'Mow', and they took it in turns to stroke her.

'That Lady Peg is very pleased,' said Jessie.

Little Miss Emily was pleased too. She smiled at the children and her big cat. Presently they stopped playing with Lady Peg, and went over to watch her stitching.

She stitched with gold thread on a small piece of dark blue cloth.

Jessie said, 'Who is that for, Miss Emily?' and Miss Emily said, 'That's for a very high-up admiral, that is, and very smart he'll look too.'

Miss Emily laughed. She had a funny old scratchy

laugh. She said, 'I like to think of my needlework going round the world and up in the air on all those well-set-up gentlemen. I feel very proud when I think of that.'

And when Joe and Timothy and Jessie thought about it, they decided that they would feel proud too, if they were Miss Emily.

They watched a little more, and the old lady stitched and stitched. Then Jessie said, 'Well, I think we'll be off now. Goodbye, Miss Emily.'

'Goodbye, dearie,' said the old lady.

'Goodbye, Lady Peg,' the children called, but the smoky-blue pussy was too busy licking herself to say anything.

It was great fun going up to Jessie's landing again. They talked and talked about the funny old lady and her big, hungry cat.

'I like living here,' said Joe. 'It's such fun in a house where there are so many people!'

Out with the Dads

Joe's Mum and Timothy's Mum are very nice ladies. They are usually very good-tempered and very kind, but, of course, like everyone else they get cross sometimes.

One Sunday morning Timothy's mother was cross.

First she was cross because she couldn't find one of her slippers, and then she was cross with the milkman for leaving the milk up on the roadway instead of bringing it down the steps to her door. That meant she had to go all the way up to the pavement to fetch it for the family breakfast.

After that she was cross because some people went past when she was collecting it, and saw her with her hair in rollers.

Then she shouted at Alfie the cat because he ran down the steps in front of her making 'mee-ows' at the bottles. Alfie is always excited when he sees the milk-bottles and usually Timothy's Mum laughs at him, so he was very surprised when she shouted.

He was so surprised that he ran and hid himself behind the dustbins, and wouldn't come out even though Timothy called and called to him.

Timothy's Dad had been having a shave, but he came out with his face all soapy when he heard the shouting and was just in time to see poor Alfie run behind the dustbins. He thought it was very funny and he began to laugh so that Timothy's Mum got cross with *him*.

But, when he saw Alfie's black face peeping out from behind the dustbins and Timothy crouching down to talk to him he laughed again, and he laughed so much and looked so funny laughing with his soapy face that Timothy's mother stopped being cross and began to laugh as well.

Then Timothy laughed too!

They all went indoors laughing, and, while his Dad finished his shave, Timothy's Mum cooked a special Sunday breakfast of fishcakes and tomatoes for them.

While they were eating it Alfie jumped in through the kitchen window and began to rub himself against Timothy's mother's legs in the most friendly way, asking for *his* fish-cake – just as if there hadn't been any shouting at all!

Timothy's Mum had it all ready for him. She gave him a saucer of milk too.

She said, 'Poor old Alfie! I don't know what came over me. I felt as cross as two sticks!'

His Dad said, 'Never mind. I expect you were tired. I know,' Timothy's Dad said, 'I'll take young Timothy off your hands for the morning! We will go for a walk in the Park and you can have a bit of a rest before dinner.'

And that is just what happened.

Off went Timothy and his father: up the steps to the roadway; down the pavement to the High Street; over the road at the traffic lights – off to the Park!

It was the very first time Timothy had ever been to the Park on a Sunday morning, and the very first time he had ever been out with his Daddy on his own, and everything seemed different.

There were people in the Park Timothy had never seen before – quite a lot of fathers out with their children; and everyone seemed to have lots of time to walk about and look at things.

Timothy and his father often stopped to look, and although Timothy had seen all the things in the Park before, they seemed much more interesting when his Daddy pointed them out to him.

They stopped at the little pond and watched some big boys sailing boats, and his father told him that it was the wind that sent the boats along by blowing in their sails. Timothy had never heard that before.

Now he stood and watched, and when he felt the breeze touch his face, he saw the little boats going faster and faster.

Presently the boats stayed quite still and the big boys threw stones at them and tried to make waves in the water to move them.

Timothy said, 'The wind has stopped, hasn't it, Dad?' and his Dad said, 'Yes, that's right, Tim.'

When they got to the middle of the Park where the fountains throw up the water in summertime his Dad showed him some big baskets under the water. He said they were full of lily-roots and that the big goldfish liked to sleep in them.

Timothy got down as low as he could to see if he could see any goldfish and so did his father, but they couldn't see anything except stones and darkness.

And then, while they were looking, someone said, 'Hello, Timothy!'

It was Joe with *his* Daddy. They were out for a walk in the Park too!

Timothy was pleased to see his friend. He showed him the baskets under the water and told him about the yellow water-lilies that would grow out of them later on, and about the goldfish, and Joe was very interested. While the two friends talked to each other their fathers talked too.

Presently they all walked along together, the two fathers talking and laughing just like Joe and Timothy's mothers talked when they met in the Park, while the little boys ran along beside them pretending to be racing-cars.

After a while the fathers stopped talking and played games with Joe and Timothy. They chased them and lifted them up in the air when they caught them. They gave them rides on their shoulders and ran races on the grass.

It was fun!

Joe said, 'Our Dads are very strong, Timothy.'

Then Joe's Dad jumped right over a rope that was hanging on posts all round a part of the grass, and then Timothy's father jumped over it too. And a Park-keeper shouted at them – just as if they had been naughty boys!

Joe and Timothy laughed when the keeper grumbled at their Daddies.

Joe's Dad said, 'You'd better not tell your mothers!' and they laughed again.

Then they all went to the café near the Park gates and had something to drink. The two fathers had tea but Joe and Timothy had hot chocolate with froth on the top. They had never had it before and they said it was lovely.

While they were drinking their chocolate, Timothy said, 'Look Joe, look! There is the Special Lady going by!'

And so she was, their very own Special Lady! She had an orange hat on today, and an orange handbag and clickety-clackety orange shoes. She saw the little boys looking out of the café window and she waved to them. Joe and Timothy waved back.

Their fathers were very surprised to think that they had such a smart Special Lady for a friend.

When they had finished their hot drinks, they all went back home together to the tall house.

Joe and his Dad went up, up, up the stairs to their home among the chimney-pots where Joe's mother was waiting with their Sunday dinner. They were very hungry. They had meat and potatoes and cabbage and apple-pie and custard and they ate every bit!

Timothy and his father went down the steps from the pavement to their home at the bottom of the tall house.

Timothy's mother was waiting for them, and so was Alfie who wanted his dinner. They had meat pie and potatoes and parsnips and orange jelly with cream, and they ate all their dinner up too.

While they were eating Timothy and his Dad told his mother all about their happy morning in the Park, and she said, 'It looks as if I shall have to be cross on a Sunday morning more often. You have enjoyed yourselves so much!'

Timothy has a surprise

Timothy, the little boy who lives at the bottom of the big house, lives so low down that he has to go up steps to get to the little yard where his Mum hangs her washing. There is a sort of shed-cupboard place under those steps – and it's a good thing there is, too, because Timothy's Dad can keep his bike in there, and there is room for some of the other things that his mother hasn't a place for indoors.

Well now, one day Timothy saw his mother poking and pulling about in that useful place, moving things and grumbling because everything was in such a muddle.

'Oh dear,' she was saying, 'I shall have to wait for Daddy to come home, after all!'

She said, 'I am trying to get your old cot out, but it's all tangled up with this chair that Daddy is going to mend and some firewood and some paint-pots, so I shall just have to wait.'

Now Timothy was very surprised when his mother said this, because he had quite forgotten about his old cot. He slept in a big boy's bed now.

He was even more surprised when his Mum said, 'We shall want that cot for the new baby.'

Timothy's mother went indoors again then, and made two cups of cocoa, one for Timothy and one for herself; and while they were drinking it she told him that quite soon they were going to have another little child to live with them – a nice little baby brother or sister for Timothy!

She said, 'The little baby is growing inside me at the moment – in a very nice safe warm place, but it will soon be wanting to come out to meet its brother, Timothy!'

Timothy *was* excited to hear about the new baby.

He knew that lots of other children had baby brothers and sisters, but he had never thought that he would be so lucky.

His Mum said, 'When the new baby comes, I will push your bed right up against the wall to make room for the cot, as the baby will have to sleep in your room.'

Timothy listened and listened and tried to think just what it would be like to have a real live kicking baby in a cot sleeping in his little room, but he just couldn't!

He said, 'Can I go and see Joe, Mum? I want to tell Joe!'

His Mum laughed and said, 'All right then, only be a good boy, and go straight upstairs, mind!'

So off went Timothy; up and up the stairs to visit his friend Joe. He hurried and hurried.

He went right past the landing where Jessie lived, but he forgot to look to see if she was there, he was so excited.

When he got up to the very top of the tall house, and came to the door of Joe's home, he hurried so much he was quite out of breath, and his legs felt so tired he had to sit on the floor while he knocked on the door.

He was so low down that Joe's mother couldn't think what was knocking. She opened the door in a very surprised way – and nearly fell over him!

'Goodness,' said Joe's Mum. 'Here's young Timothy! Why, he looks as if he has been running in a race.'

When Joe heard this, he came rushing out, and pulled Timothy up, and pushed him inside because he could see at once that Timothy had something *very special* to tell him.

At last Timothy said, 'Joe,' in a little, puffy voice, 'Joe, I am going to have a little baby brother or a little baby sister. It's safe and warm inside my Mum, Joe, but it wants to come out to see me.'

Joe was so surprised to hear this that his mouth went O and his eyes went O.

But Joe's Mum said, 'Yes, that's right. Timothy's Mummy is going to the hospital to have the new baby, and while she is at the hospital, Timothy is going to live up here with us.'

That was another surprise for Joe and Timothy!

Joe's Mum said, 'The lady underneath is going to lend me a folding bed. I shall push Joe's bed right up into the corner to make room for it, and Timothy will sleep on it.'

She said, 'Timothy's Dad said he would carry Timothy's bed up, but it's a long way, all up those stairs. I think the folding bed idea is much nicer.'

Well, well! All these plans had been going on and Joe and Timothy hadn't known about them!

They could hardly believe it was really going to happen. First the baby, and then Timothy to sleep in a strange folding bed in Joe's little room!

They went downstairs to tell Jessie. She came out at once as soon as they came to her landing. She had seen Timothy hurrying by, because she had been peeping out of her letterbox, and she had guessed there was something exciting happening.

Jessie was very interested when the boys told her about the baby, because, although she had brothers and sisters, she hadn't got a baby one – she was the baby herself; at least, her Mum said she was, though Jessie thinks she is a big girl.

After that Timothy kept saying, 'When am I going to sleep in Joe's room? *When* am I going to stay with Joe's Mum?' and Joe kept saying, '*When* is Timothy's baby brother or sister coming? When will Timothy sleep in the folding bed in my little room?'

But all Timothy's Mum and Joe's Mum could say was, 'We really don't quite know. Babies come when they are ready and not before – you will just have to wait.'

And that was just what they had to do. But they talked and talked and got so excited and fidgetty that Joe's Mum took them to the Park to play.

When they got to the Park the Special Lady was there, so they told *her* all about it and she was so pleased she taught all the children to sing 'Hush-a-bye baby,' because she said Timothy might find that a useful song to know.

You would think all these surprises would be enough for Timothy, wouldn't you? A baby coming – a stay with Joe in the home among the chimney-pots – a folding bed – a new song for the baby; but that wasn't all!

The BIG SURPRISE was this: one morning Timothy woke up, and the first thing he *didn't* see was his own little bedroom wall with his own picture of a boat and a lighthouse that he knew so well. The first thing he *didn't* see was his mother smiling and saying, 'Get up, it's time for breakfast.'

Instead he saw a strange wall of a strange little bedroom with a picture of a big dog and a little dog on it; and he saw his own friend Joe in another bed, looking at him in a very surprised way.

'How did you get here?'

'How did I get here?'

They both said this at the same time.

Timothy remembered going to sleep in his own bed downstairs! They were both excited then. They jumped up and down on their beds and shouted, until Joe's Mum came in and told them to be quiet.

'You'll wake all the neighbours,' she said, but she was smiling all the same.

'But how did I get here?' asked Timothy.

'He wasn't here when I went to sleep,' cried Joe.

'His Daddy brought him upstairs last night,' said Joe's Mum. 'He rolled him up in a blanket and carried him up all those stairs! It's a very long way, and he had to stop once or twice to get his breath back, but Timothy never woke up! He knocked on our door, and Timothy didn't wake up, and we put him into this bed, but he didn't wake up; and you didn't wake up either, Joe. You're a pair of dreamers, that's what you are!'

How Joe and Timothy laughed. 'It *is* a surprise,' said Timothy.

'There's another surprise,' said Joe's mother. 'The little baby arrived last night – it is in the Hospital with your Mummy, Timothy. You have a little baby SISTER!'

Three fathers

Timothy's Dad works outside, just like Joe's Dad, but he doesn't lay pipes in the road. He works for the builders who make the very big buildings for shops and offices and factories.

As for Jessie's Dad – he is a bus conductor. Sometimes he has to start very early in the morning so that he can get home early, but at other times he doesn't go to work until quite late and has to come home at a very late time, long after the children in the tall house are in bed.

But you always know when he is at home in the day-time, because he is always laughing and singing. He has a very dark brown face so that when he laughs his teeth look very white, and he looks so jolly everyone laughs as well.

Joe's and Timothy's Dads often travel on Jessie's Dad's bus, so they are very good friends. They call him Ernie.

Now, Joe has a dear old Country Gran and he likes to visit her very much. There is a man called Mr Lemon who lives in the tall, tall house and he drives a lorry and sometimes he goes out to where Joe's Gran lives. When he does he takes Joe and his Mum so that they can visit the dear old lady. But they have to come home by bus because Mr Lemon can't wait all day for them.

Well now, one day, while Timothy was staying in the upstairs home with Joe, Mr Lemon said he was going out through the village where Joe's Gran lived. He said he could take Joe and Timothy and Joe's mother if they liked to come. He said he thought he could make room for Jessie too!

Wasn't that kind of him?

Joe's Mum said she thought it would be a very nice idea. She knew Country Gran would not mind how many children she brought with her.

Jessie's mother said that she could go and so, while Mr Lemon went to fetch his lorry, they were all tidied up for the journey; and when they climbed into the lorry at last they looked the neatest, brightest children in the street, and everyone came out to wave them goodbye.

It was a lovely trip: right out into the country. Mr

Lemon had to stop sometimes and leave parcels at shops and hotels on the way, so they had plenty of things to see and talk about.

When they came to Country Gran's house she was very pleased to see them. She had a flowery garden with chickens and bees and vegetables in it.

While they were admiring her flowers and peeping at her hens she made them a lovely dinner of fried eggs and bacon and cake and bread and jam.

After dinner Joe and Timothy and Jessie went and played in a field behind the house while Joe's Mum talked to dear Country Gran.

Then there was just time for a cup of tea and some biscuits before they set off for home.

First they had to go down the lane where Joe's Gran lived and wait on a corner for a little green bus which took them for an up and down and round and round through the lanes ride, and then went down and down to a big red town.

That was the end of the journey for the little green bus. So they got out and waited at a bus stop for a big green bus. While they waited they talked and laughed and watched the people going by with heavy baskets full of shopping, and vans loaded with sheep and pigs and chicken. Someone told Joe's mother that it was Market Day.

When at last the big bus came they climbed up to the top because they still had a long way to go, and Joe's Mum said they would get a nice view upstairs.

And what do you think? Upstairs, all ready to ring the bell, with his nice face smiling to see them, was Jessie's Dad!

'Well, well,' he said. 'I never thought to see you on my bus!'

It was lovely travelling on Jessie's Dad's bus. All the travellers knew him, and he made them laugh. He told them that his little girl and her friends were upstairs, so that all the upstairs travellers looked round to see them, and all the downstairs people looked up at them when they got off at their bus stops!

Whenever he wasn't selling tickets, and talking to his friends the travellers, Jessie's father came up to talk to the children and point out all sorts of things on the way.

Presently the bus came to a place where a big building was going up and where big cranes were moving up and down. Jessie's Dad pointed. 'Look, Timothy,' he said, 'that's where your Dad works. See?'

Then he pointed again. 'There he is!' he cried. 'Right up there in his yellow jacket!'

And there, right up on the side of the building, high among the scaffolding, was Timothy's Dad. How Timothy shouted and waved. His Dad couldn't see him, of course, he was too high up, but Timothy waved anyway.

When the bus got further along they came to a place where a long line of workmen were laying long red pipes in the ground.

'Why,' said Joe's mother to Joe, 'there's *your* Daddy, Joe – look! Look!'

And there was Joe's Daddy working hard with the other men! Joe's Mum tapped the window, and Joe waved hard and his Daddy looked up and saw them. He *did* smile.

When the bus came to the stop nearest to their road they all got off and stood waving 'Goodbye' to Jessie's Daddy until he was out of sight.

'What a lovely day,' said Timothy. 'To think I have seen my Dad working! When I am a big man I want to climb high up like he does, and build places.'

'I liked seeing my Daddy too,' said Joe. 'I think when I

grow up I will be a workman like him. I will put poles with red lights on them all down the road and the people going by will talk to me.'

'I am going to be a bus conductor lady one day,' said Jessie, 'because my Dad says that's the best job of all, helping people on to the bus and making them laugh.'

The children were so pleased to think they had seen their Daddies at work, they decided to watch out of the landing window where they could see the corner of the street, to see which father came home first.

But that day, as it happened, Jessie's Daddy was just

coming down from the Garage when he saw Joe's Dad and Timothy's Dad coming down the road, so he joined them and as they walked he told them how the children had seen them working at their jobs. He told them in such a funny way, that they both laughed and laughed and they were all laughing as they came round the corner together.

So Joe and Timothy and Jessie laughed to see them, and were still laughing as they ran down the stairs to meet them at the door of the big house, to tell them about their day in the country.

Names

One day, while Timothy was still staying with Joe in the high-up home among the chimneys, Jessie's mother took the three children to the playground in the Park, on one of the Special Lady's days.

Jessie's Mum took them, because Joe's Mum was busy cleaning Timothy's mother's home for her before she came back from the hospital with the new baby, and, because Jessie's Mum had a lot of shopping to do that afternoon, she took them to the playground early.

The Special Lady was already there. She knows that people often bring their children early, so she takes her lunch and eats it at the playground in case anyone turns up.

She had just finished her lunch when she heard them coming round the corner of the playground wall, so she went out to meet them and say 'Hello' to them in her friendly way.

Joe said, 'Hello.'

Timothy said, 'Hello.'

But Jessie said, 'My, my, you look lovely today!' For the Special Lady had a beautiful white dress with yellow sunflowers on it, with yellow shoes to match, and little goldy ear-rings.

Jessie's mother said she was sorry to be early, but the Special Lady said, 'Don't worry about that. I have some children here already!'

She said, 'As a matter of fact, I am very pleased to see Joe and Timothy and Jessie. They can help me to entertain the two little mites – they are the sweetest little things, but I can't understand a word they say!'

The Special Lady said, 'I am sure Jessie will be able to help me – she is so good with shy children!'

The Special Lady told Jessie's mother that the two little mites were so shy, she didn't even know their names, and Jessie's mother said, 'My Jessie will look after them all right, and if anyone can find out their names, my Jessie can.'

So the children ran ahead of the Special Lady, and clever Jessie found the little mites first.

She found a dear little small boy and girl with round brown faces and dark little eyes, sitting quietly on a bench with a book that the Special Lady had found for them; and when she saw them, looking so small and so good, kind Jessie smiled and smiled at them, and the little shy children smiled back.

Jessie said, 'Hello then, are you twins, eh?'

But the little children didn't say anything.

Timothy said, 'I've got a new baby sister. Have you got a baby at home?'

But the children didn't say anything at all.

Joe said, 'Will you come for a ride on the round-and-round with us?'

But the children still didn't say anything at all, so Joe and Timothy went off and left Jessie with the shy little mites.

Presently some more children came, so the Special Lady said, as she had brought her radio with her, they might as well sit down for a bit and listen to the children's programme. She said she thought they might know some of the songs, and if they did they could sing them.

So all the early children sat down round the Special Lady's radio, and listened to the children's programme. They had the 'Grand Old Duke of York' on the children's programme, which pleased Joe and Timothy very much. They sang and sang, and the other children sang too – except the shy little mites: they only smiled.

Then Joe and Timothy got up and began to march up and down pretending to play their drums, and the other children got up and pretended too, and this time the shy little mites got up and marched and pretended to play drums!

After the music the lady on the radio told a story, and then there was another song.

This new song was about a very funny man whose name was *Aiken Drum*. Every now and again the singing lady sang,

'And he played upon a ladle, a ladle, a ladle –
He played upon a ladle
   and his name was Aiken Drum'

and it wasn't long before all the children were singing
that bit with her.

When the programme was over, Jessie said, 'I think
that's a funny name, AIKEN Drum. I think that's a
really funny name.'

Joe said, 'I don't suppose Aiken Drum thinks it's funny.'

Timothy said, 'I expect he would think Joe and
Timothy are funny names, or Peter or Georgie.'

The Special Lady said, 'No names are funny to the
people who have them.'

Then Jessie said, 'Special Lady, have you got a name?
I know you are Miss Laurence, but have you another
name too?'

The Special Lady said, 'Well, I have, as a matter of fact
– you might even think it was a funny name. My first
name is Aurora.'

The children were very surprised.

Joe and Timothy thought she said 'Roarer', like a lion
does, and didn't think they liked it for their Special Lady.

'Not Roarer,' the Special Lady said. 'Aurora. My father wanted me called that.'

The Special Lady told them that when she was a tiny brand-new baby she was born just as the sun was coming up over the chimney tops outside her mother's bedroom window.

The Special Lady said, 'My father said it was such a lovely dawn, all the clouds golden and bright. So he thought I should be called after it. Aurora is another word for dawn!'

'Well! That's another word we know,' said Joe to Timothy. 'Aurora means dawn, and dawn means the early sunshine that comes first thing in the morning. I know that, because my Daddy showed me the dawn one day when I woke up early. It's very pretty!'

The Special Lady said, 'I think the dawn is lovely too, so I am very pleased to have Aurora for my name.'

Then Jessie said, 'Are we going to play one of your nice singing games now, Special Lady? Hamid and Ayesha want to play – they like the bit when you do the actions. They like to pretend to play drums and things.'

Hamid and Ayesha? All the children looked at each other.

The Special Lady looked at Jessie. Then she looked at the shy little mites who were smiling and smiling.

'Is that what they are called? Hamid and Ayesha?' she said.

The two little mites smiled and smiled again, and nodded their little dark heads. They said some words that no one understood. Except Jessie. At least, she thought she did!

Anyway, she *had* found out their names!

The new baby sister

You can imagine the excitement there was in the tall house when Timothy's mother brought the new baby from the hospital! Even though Timothy and his father and mother live so low down and have a different way to get into the street, it was surprising how many people had got to know about the baby.

She is a nice, good little thing, and Timothy is very proud of her. But he was very surprised at all the people who came down to see the baby and who gave her presents. Some of them were people he had never seen before.

Jessie's Mum made a very great fuss when she heard that the baby was coming home. She went out and bought a lovely bunch of daffodils and a big bag of oranges for Timothy's Mum, and Jessie's big brothers and sisters all put their money together and bought a lovely pink plastic rattle with bells on it, and they all went down with their mother to give it to the baby.

Joe's Mum had knitted a sweet little white coat and bonnet and a pair of funny little bootees with pom-poms on them. She made a sponge cake too, because she thought Timothy's mother might fancy it for tea.

The lady who lent the folding bed for Timothy to sleep on came down to see the baby, and put a bright shiny ten pence piece into her little hand for luck.

Mr Lemon brought his mate in to see her, and they gave Timothy's Mum a whole pound between them, to buy the baby a present!

Timothy thought it was like a special kind of birth-day!

It was very strange having a little baby sleeping in his room. At first he didn't like it very much, because it didn't seem quite like his room any more – with the cot and everything: but after a while he liked having her. She was so very good and smiling, and she played such pretty games with her rattle that he loved to watch her.

Now he says she is the best baby in the world!

It was nice having his mother home again too, and he spent a lot of time telling her about all the things he had done and learned while she was in hospital. It was good to know she was so interested in everything he told her.

One day, when the baby was a few weeks old, Mr Lemon's lorry arrived, and on the lorry was Timothy's Dad with a bright blue pram for the baby.

Joe's Country Gran had known a lady who wanted to sell her pram because her baby had grown too big for it. It was such a bargain that Timothy's Dad had gone along with Mr Lemon to buy it!

Now in the daytime Baby could sleep in her pram in the little backyard, and now she would be taken down to the shops. When Joe and Timothy went out with the baby in the pram they held on to either side as they walked along and talked to the baby if she was awake.

Jessie liked to hold the handle and help to push.

One lovely sunny day, when all the daffodils and tulips were shining in the flower-beds in the Park, all the children were running about in the playground enjoying the spring sunshine. Timothy's Mum, Joe's Mum and Jessie's Mum, and Timothy, Joe and Jessie as well, went for a walk together through the High Street and up the Market and down the Row to the Park.

As soon as they were inside, the three children ran ahead to the playground. The three mothers came slowly after them, with the blue pram and the baby.

The Special Lady was in the playground. She had a green and white stripy jumper and green trousers, and she shouted out, 'Hello, Joe and Timothy and Jessie! It *is* nice to see you!'

They hurried up to her, and began to tell her about the baby.

'I must see her at once. I just can't wait,' the Special Lady said.

And she ran out of the playground and down the path to where the three mothers were walking with the pram. The three friends ran after her, and a lot of the playground children ran too.

It was exciting!

Baby was wide awake, and the Special Lady said she was the sweetest little thing she had ever seen.

She said, 'What is her name?'

Timothy looked at Joe, Joe looked at Timothy. They both looked at Jessie. Oh dear! What indeed?

But Timothy's mother knew at once, 'She is Dawn Gloria,' she said proudly. 'Timothy told me about your name, and as Baby was born early in the morning, just

like you were, with the dawn and everything, I thought I would call her Dawn. I didn't fancy Aurora, but I think Dawn is lovely. She is Gloria after me,' Timothy's mother said.

She said that Dawn Gloria was going to be christened soon, and, as she was a girl-baby and girl-babies had two godmothers, Joe's mother and Jessie's mother were going to be her godmothers.

That was something else Joe and Timothy hadn't known before.

'Dawn Gloria' – what a glorious sunny early-morning name! How proud Timothy felt, and when the Special Lady and the other children sang 'Hush-a-bye Baby' very softly for the new baby, he smiled and smiled.

And so did Joe, and so did Jessie. After all, the baby lived in their house, didn't she?

Fattypuffs and Thinifers

ANDRÉ MAUROIS

Edmund loved food and was plump, but his brother Terry was very thin, and when they took a moving staircase to the Country Under the Earth, they found themselves split up and in the midst of the dispute between the Fattypuffs and the Thinifers.

My Naughty Little Sister
My Naughty Little Sister's Friends
When My Naughty Little Sister Was Good

DOROTHY EDWARDS

These now famous stories were originally told by a mother to her own children. Ideal for reading aloud. For ages 4 to 8.

Five Dolls in a House

HELEN CLARE

A little girl called Elizabeth finds a way of making herself small and visits her dolls in their own house. Girls.

Flat Stanley

JEFF BROWN AND TOMI UNGERER

Stanley Lambchop was an ordinary boy, except for one thing: he was four feet tall, about a foot wide, and only half an inch thick!